JEAN DE BRUNHOFF

THE TRAVELS
of
BABAR

Translated from the French by Merle Haas
Harrison Smith & Robert Haas
New York 1934
Random House, New York, 1985

In
the same series :

The Story of Babar

the little elephant ,

in which are told
his earlier
adventures.

Babar, the young King of the elephants,
and his wife, Queen Céleste,
have just left for their wedding trip
in a balloon.
"Good-bye! See you soon!"
cry the elephants
as they watch the balloon rise and drift away.
Arthur, Babar's little cousin,
still waves his beret.
Old Cornelius, who is chief over all the elephants
when the King is away, anxiously sighs:
"I do hope they won't have any accidents!"

The country of the elephants is now far away.
The balloon glides noiselessly in the sky.
Babar and Céleste admire the landscape below.
What a beautiful journey!
The air is balmy, the wind is gentle.
There is the ocean, the big blue ocean.

Blown out over the sea by the wind,
the balloon is suddenly caught
by a violent storm.
Babar and Céleste tremble with fear
and cling with all their might to the basket
of the balloon.

By extraordinary good fortune,
just as the balloon
was about to fall
into the sea,
a final puff of wind
blows it on an island
where it flattens out and collapses.
"You aren't hurt, Céleste, are you?"
Babar inquires anxiously.
"No! Well then look, we are saved!"

Leaving the wrecked balloon on the beach,
Babar and Céleste pick up their belongings
and go off to seek shelter.
Having found a quiet spot,
they take off their clothes.
Céleste hangs them up on a line to dry,
while Babar lights a good fire
and prepares breakfast.

Babar and Céleste settle themselves comfortably.
They have set up their tent,
and sitting on some large stones,
they eat with relish
an excellent rice broth
well-sweetened and cooked to perfection.
"We are not so badly off on this island,"
says Babar.

After breakfast,
while Babar explores the surrounding country,
Céleste, left alone,
has fallen sound asleep.
Just then,
the inhabitants of the island,
fierce and savage cannibals,
suddenly discover her.
"What kind of strange beast is this?"
they say to eachother,
"We have never seen anything like it.
Its meat must be very tender.
Let's creep up quietly and catch it
while it sleeps."

The cannibals have succeeded in tying up Céleste
with the clothes line
on which the clothes were drying.
Some dance with joy, while others have great fun
trying on the stolen garments.
Céleste sighs sadly,
she thinks soon she will be eaten.
She does not yet see Babar, who returns
just in time to save her!

In the twinkling of an eye, Babar has unbound Céleste.
They both hurl themselves on the cannibals.
Some are wounded, others take flight;
All are terrified.

Only a few courageous ones still resist.
But they are thinking:
" These big animals are certainly terribly strong
and their hides are mighty tough! "

After having chased off the savages,
Babar and Céleste rest themselves on the seashore.
Suddenly, right in front of them
a whale comes to the surface and spouts.
Babar gets up immediately and says:
"Good morning, Mrs. Whale,
I am Babar King of the elephants
and here is my wife Céleste.
We have had a balloon accident
and have fallen here on this island.
Could you help us to get away?"

" I am delighted
to make your acquaintance, "
answers the whale,
" and I will be very happy
if I can be of service to you.
I am just leaving to visit my family
in the Arctic Ocean.
I will drop you wherever you like.
Quick, get on my back
and hold tight so you don't slip off.
Are you ready ? Get set. Let's go ! "

A few days later, a little weary,
they are resting on a reef.
Just then a school of little fish swam by.
"I am going to eat up some of these,"
said the whale.
"I'll be back in a minute."
And she dives down after them.

The whale has not come back !!!
While eating the little fish,
She completely forgot her new friends.
She is a giddy, thoughtless creature.
"We were better off on the cannibal island.
What will become of us now?" weeps poor Céleste.
Babar does his best to comfort her.

After hours and hours
spent on their little reef,
without even a drop of fresh water,
they finally spy a ship
passing quite near them.
She is a big steamer
with three funnels.
Babar and Céleste call out
and yell as loudly as they can,
but no one hears them.
They try signaling with their trunks
and with their arms.
Oh, will they attract someone's attention?

They have been seen ! A life boat rescues them
while the excited passengers all watch.

A week later, the huge ship

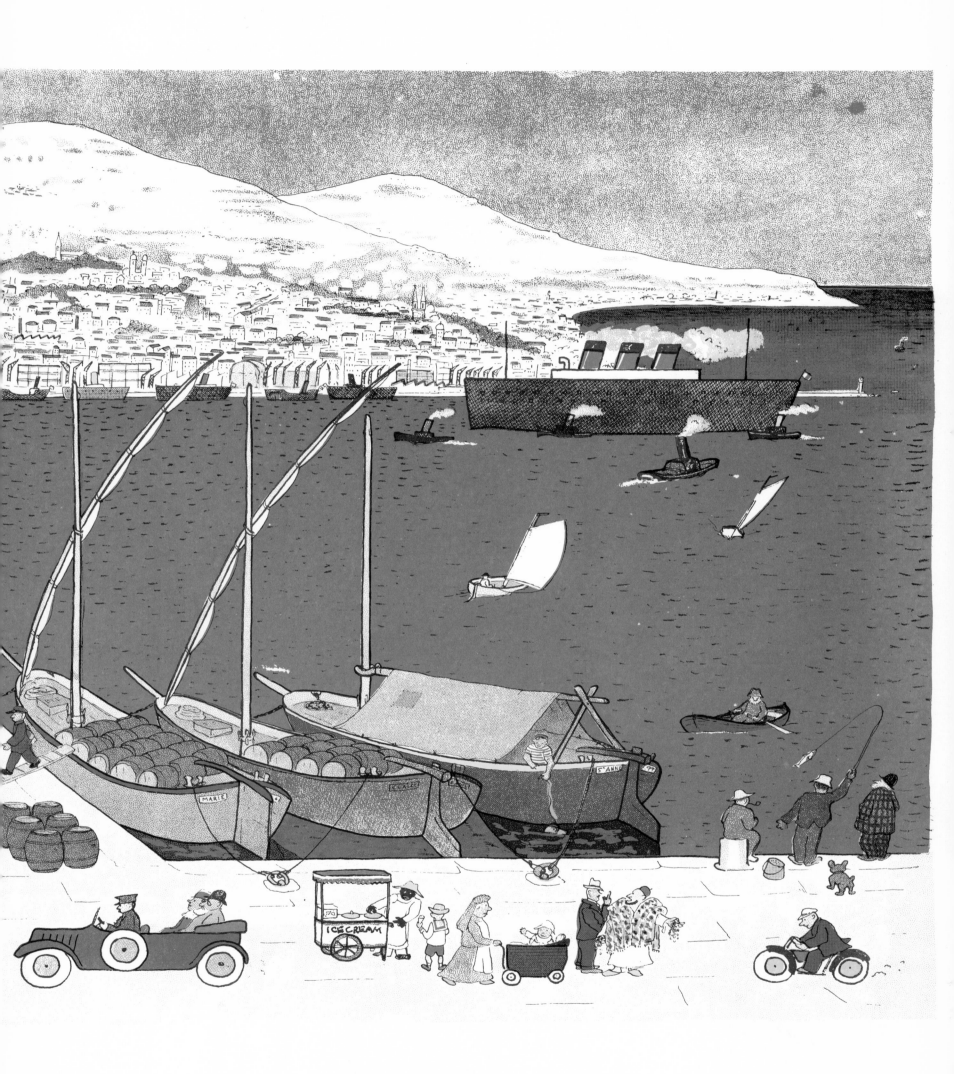

steams slowly into a big harbor.

All the passengers go down the gangplank.
Babar and Céleste, too, would like to follow
but they are not allowed to.
They have lost their crowns
during the storm,
so no one will believe
that they are actually King and Queen of the elephants,
and the Captain of the ship
orders them locked up in the ship's stables.

"They give us straw to sleep on!"
cries Babar angrily.
"We are fed hay, as though we were donkeys!
The door is locked!
I've had enough of this, I'm going to smash everything."
"Be quiet, I beg you," says Céleste,
"I hear some one. It is the Captain
coming into the stable.
Let's be good so he'll let us out."

"Here are my elephants,"
says the Captain
to the famous animal trainer, Fernando,
who is with him.
"I cannot keep them on my ship;
I give them to you for your circus."

Fernando thanks the Captain
and leads away his two new pupils.
"Be patient, Babar," whispers Céleste,
"We will not remain long with the circus.
We will get back to our native land again somehow
and see Cornelius and little Arthur."

Now just at this time,
back in the elephants' country,
little Arthur has had a mischievous idea.
While Rataxes the rhinoceros
was having a quiet siesta,
Arthur tied a big fire-cracker to his tail
without waking him.
The fire-cracker explodes with a terrific bang
and Rataxes leaps up into the air.
Arthur, the scamp,
laughs until he nearly chokes.
It is really a very mean trick.

Rataxes is furious.
Cornelius, very worried, goes to find him and says:
"My dear fellow, I am so sorry.
Arthur will be severely punished.
He begs for your forgiveness."
"Get away, old Cornelius," grumbles Rataxes.
"Don't speak to me of that scoundrel, Arthur.
You elephants may think you have made fun of me
but just wait, — you'll soon see!"
"What will he do?" wonders Cornelius.
"I feel very uneasy; he is revengeful and mean.
Ah! If only Babar were here!"

But Babar is now far away playing the trumpet

while Céleste dances in Fernando's circus.

One day the circus comes to the town
where Babar, when he was young,
had met his friend the old lady.
So, at night, while Fernando is in bed,
Babar and Céleste escape and go to find her,
for he has never forgotten her.

Babar finds the house easily
and rings the bell.
The old lady awakes,
puts on her wrapper, steps out on her balcony
and calls: "Who's there?"
"It is Babar and Céleste," they answer her.

The old lady is overjoyed.
She has really believed
she would never see them again.
Babar and Céleste are happy, too,
for they will never have to go back to the circus.
Soon they will be able to rejoin Arthur and Cornelius.
The old lady has promised to help them.

The old lady lends Céleste a night-gown
and a pair of pajamas to Babar.
They have just awakened
after a sound sleep.
Now they are having breakfast in bed
for they are still quite tired
after all their adventures.

At the circus,
their escape has just been discovered.
" Stop ! Thief ! My elephants have been stolen ! "
crys the excited Fernando.
" Little ones, oh little ones, where are you hiding ? "
the clowns repeat, and look everywhere for them.

Babar and Céleste
will not be caught again.
Here they are on their way to the station
with the old lady.
They need a few days rest
before returning to their own land.
So the three of them
are going to the mountains to enjoy the fresh air
and try a little skiing.

Now Babar and Céleste
have packed away their skiis
and said good-bye to the mountains.
They are leaving by plane
to return home.
The old lady accompanies them.
Babar has invited her,
as he is anxious to show her his beautiful country
and the great forest
where one always hears the birds singing.

They have landed.
The aeroplane has gone back.
Babar and Céleste are speechless with surprise.
Where are Cornelius, Arthur and the other elephants?
A few broken trees!
Is that all that is left of the great forest?
There are no more flowers, no more birds.
Babar and Céleste are very sad and weep
as they see their ruined country.
The old lady understands their grief.

"What is going on here?" inquires Babar,
who has found the other elephants at last.
"Alas!" replies Cornelius,
"The rhinoceroses have declared war on us.
They came led by Rataxes
who wanted to catch Arthur
and make mince-meat of him!
We tried bravely to protect the little fellow,
but the rhinoceroses were too strong for us.
We do not know how to drive them off."
"This is indeed bad news," says Babar,
"but let's not give up."

But real war is not a joke,
and many of the elephants have been wounded.
Céleste and the old lady
take care of them with great devotion.
The old lady is especially good at this,
as she used to be a trained nurse.
Babar has gone back to the front with Cornelius
and some of the soldiers who have recovered
to join the elephant army.
The rhinoceroses are preparing to attack.
A big battle will soon begin!

Here is the camp of the rhinoceroses.
The soldiers are awaiting orders, and think:
" We will once again defeat the elephants,
then the war will be over
and we can all go home."
Spiteful old Rataxes
maliciously says to his friend General Pamir:
" Hah! Hah! Hah! Pretty soon
we will tweak the ears of this young King Babar
and punish that rascal Arthur."

Here is the camp of the elephants.
They have all found new courage.
And now Babar has a bright idea:
He disguises his biggest soldiers,
    painting their tails bright red,
and near their tails on either side
    he paints large, frightening eyes.
Arthur sets to work making wigs.
    He works as hard as he can
So he'll be forgiven for causing all this trouble.

The day of the battle, at just the right moment
the disguised elephants come out of hiding.
And Babar's bright idea succeeds!

The rhinoceroses think they are monsters
and, terrified, they retreat in great disorder.
King Babar is a mighty fine general.

The rhinoceroses have fled and are still running.
Pamir and Rataxes are prisoners,
and hang their heads in shame.
What a glorious day for the elephants!
In chorus they all cry: " Bravo Babar, - Bravo!
Victory! Victory!
The war is over! How perfectly splendid! "

The next day before all the elephants,
Babar and Céleste, having put on their royal garments
and their new crowns,
reward the old lady who has been so good to them
and has cared so well for the wounded.
They give her eleven singing canaries
and a cunning little monkey.

After the ceremony,
Babar, Céleste and the old lady
sit and chat under the palm trees.
"And what are we going to do next?"
asks the old lady.
"I am going to try to rule my kingdom wisely,"
answers Babar,
"And if you will remain with us,
you can help me make my subjects
happy."

THE END